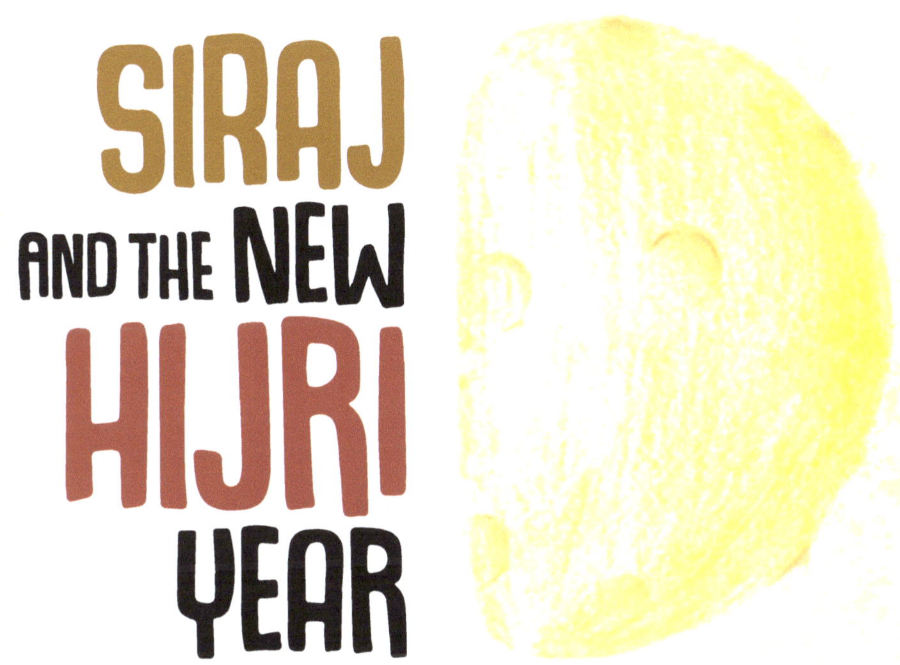

SIRAJ AND THE NEW HIJRI YEAR

Written By
Amani Jamal

Designed by:

CHY Illustration & Design

Name: ____

Publisher: Green Fig
Pennsylvania, USA
www.gogreenfig.com
info@gogreenfig.com

Siraj and the New Hijri Year - First edition
ISBN: 978-1953836953

DEAR PARENTS AND EDUCATORS,

The Hijri calendar is an important part of Islamic heritage, marking the passage of time through the lunar months and commemorating key events in history. Yet, many children today are more familiar with the Gregorian calendar and may not fully understand the significance of the Hijri year.

In **Siraj and the New Hijri Year**, young readers join Siraj on a fun and engaging journey as he learns about the twelve months of the Hijri calendar, the phases of the moon, and the meaning of the Hijrah, the migration that shaped Islamic history. Through hands-on learning and a school celebration, Siraj discovers that the Hijri year is not just about counting months but about remembering meaningful events and understanding the importance of time.

This book encourages children to appreciate their Islamic identity while developing a deeper connection to history, faith, and the world around them. Parents and educators can use this story to spark discussions about the Hijri calendar, the lunar cycle, and how we mark the passage of time in different cultures.

May this journey through time inspire curiosity and appreciation for our rich Islamic heritage.

CONTENTS

CHAPTER 1

SCHOOL PREPARATION FOR THE NEW HIJRI YEAR

It was an exciting time at school! The students were preparing to celebrate the arrival of a new Hijri year. In art class, students made colorful origami lanterns, and Miss Salma handed out big crescent shapes for each student to color and hang up in the classroom.

LEARNING GEM:

What does AH mean in the Islamic Calendar?

A.H. means 'After Hijrah'. It is used to count the years in the Islamic calendar starting from the time Prophet Muḥammad migrated from Makkah to Madinah (Al-Hijrah). When we say the year is 1448, it means that 1448 lunar years have passed since that important journey.
So, the year in which the Hijrah took place is known as 1 AH.

In science class,
Miss Sarah gave them
an assignment related to
the occasion. Each pair of
students had to make a poster showing the
phases of the moon, which determines the Hijri
months. Siraj and his best friend, Omar, were
thrilled to be assigned as
partners! They
immediately started
discussing how they
would design their
poster. Siraj could'nt wait
to go home and tell his
parents all about the
exciting day at school.

LEARNING GEM:

Did you know that both the sun and the moon move in their own orbit?
Allah said in the Qur'an:

{وَهُوَ الَّذِي خَلَقَ اللَّيْلَ وَالنَّهَارَ وَالشَّمْسَ وَالْقَمَرَ كُلٌّ فِي فَلَكٍ يَسْبَحُونَ} سورة الأنبياء / 33

Which means:
"And He is the One who created the night and the day, and the sun and the moon. Each is swimming in its own orbit."

CHAPTER 2

SIRAJ LEARNS THE MEANING OF "HIJRAH"

When Siraj got home, a delicious smell led him straight to the kitchen. His mom was baking a chicken pie.

"As-salamu–'alaykum Mom!" Siraj greeted her.

"Wa-'alaykum as-salam, Siraj. How was your day?" she replied with a warm smile.

Siraj eagerly told her about all about the activities at school. Later, he helped set the dinner table and mixed the salad.

LEARNING GEM:

The Du'a for Entering
the House

بِسْمِ اللَّهِ وَلَجْنَا، وَبِسْمِ اللَّهِ خَرَجْنَا،
وَعَلَى اللَّهِ رَبِّنَا تَوَكَّلْنَا.

Narrated by Abu Dawud

⭐ Meaning:
"In the name of Allah, we enter, and in the
name of Allah, we leave, and upon our
Lord, we place our trust."

Over dinner, Siraj asked, "Dad, what does Hijri mean?"

His father explained, "The word 'Hijri' comes from the Arabic word Hijrah, which means migration. It refers to the time when Prophet Muḥammad migrated from Makkah to Al-Madinah."

He continued, "After the Prophet's passing, the Muslims decided to make a calendar. They chose the Hijrah as the starting point because it was a very important event in the Prophet's life and in the spread of Islam.

Later that evening, Siraj's mom read to him from a book about the Seerah, the life of Prophet Muḥammad. She also promised to take him to the craft store over the weekend to buy materials and paints supplies for his school project. Siraj lay down peacefully on his right side, resting his hand under his right cheek. As he whispered his dhikr, these were the last words he said before drifting off to sleep.

LEARNING GEM:

The Last Words Before Sleeping

اللَّهُمَّ أَسْلَمْتُ نَفْسِي إِلَيْكَ، وَأَلْجَأْتُ ظَهْرِي إِلَيْكَ، وَوَجَّهْتُ وَجْهِي إِلَيْكَ، وَفَوَّضْتُ أَمْرِي إِلَيْكَ، رَغْبَةً وَرَهْبَةً إِلَيْكَ، لَا مَلْجَأَ وَلَا مَنْجَى مِنْكَ إِلَّا إِلَيْكَ، آمَنْتُ بِكِتَابِكَ الَّذِي أَنْزَلْتَ، وَبِنَبِيِّكَ الَّذِي أَرْسَلْتَ.

Narrated by al-Bukhari and Muslim

★ Simplified Meaning:
"O Allah, I submit myself to You, trust You completely, and turn to You with hope and fear. There is no safety except with You. I believe in Your Book which You have revealed, and in Your Prophet whom You have sent."

CHAPTER 3

SIRAJ IN THE RELIGIOUS EDUCATION CLASS AT SCHOOL

Trin Trin! Trin Trin!

The bell rang loudly, signaling the end of the morning break and the start of the third class. It was time for the religious education class.

The teacher, Mr Daniel, began with a quick review of the names of the twelve months of the Hijri calendar. To his delight, the entire class knew them by heart!

Then Mr Daniel explained why it's important to keep track of this calendar. "Many important things, like fasting Ramadan and performing Hajj are determined by the Hijri calendar," he said. "Other rulings also depends on it.

For example, a person becomes accountable when they reach 15 years according to the Hijri calendar."

At this, Siraj raised his hand and asked, "Isn't the age the same in both the Hijri and the calendar we use every day?"

Mr. Daniel smiled and replied, "No, Siraj, it's not the same. The Hijri calendar is shorter than the one we use everyday. You get older faster in the Hijri calendar."

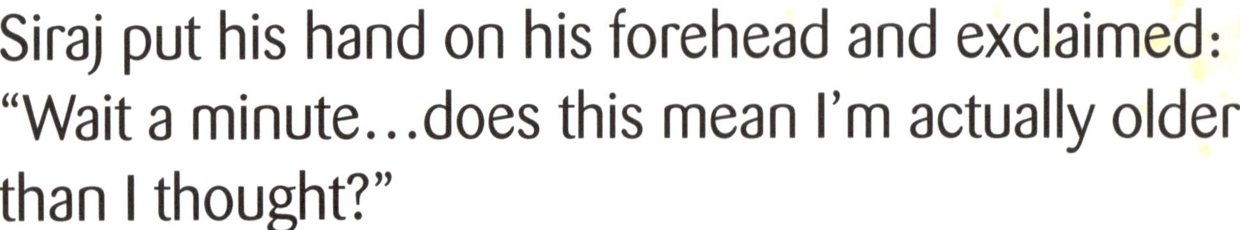

Siraj put his hand on his forehead and exclaimed: "Wait a minute…does this mean I'm actually older than I thought?"

His teacher smiled and continued: "The calendar we use every day is called the Gregorian calendar. It's based on the sun and has solar months, like January and February, while the Hijri calendar uses lunar months. Lunar months are either 29 or 30 days long, while the solar months are 30 or 31 days except for February. This means a lunar year is about 11 days shorter than a solar year. That's why Ramadan and Hajj don't fall on the same date each year."

Siraj listened carefully and began wondering what 15 lunar years would correspond to in the solar calendar. He made a mental note to figure it out later.

LEARNING GEM:

The 12 Months of the Hijri Calendar Are:

Al-Muḥarram
المُحَرَّم

Ṣafar
صَفَر

Rabi'unil-Awwal
رَبِيعٌ الأول

Rabi'unil-Ākhir
رَبِيعٌ الآخِر

Jumādal-'Ulā
جُمَادىٰ الأولىٰ

Jumādal-'Ākhirah
جُمَادىٰ الآخِرة

Rajab
رَجَب

Sha'bān
شَعبان

Ramaḍān
رَمَضان

Shawwāl
شَوَّال

Dhul-Qa'dah
ذو القَعدة

Dhul-Ḥijjah
ذو الحِجَّة

CHAPTER 4

SIRAJ AND OMAR WORK ON THEIR MOON PHASES POSTER

The weekend had finally arrived, and Siraj was excited. His mom had promised to take him and his sister, Noor, to the craft supplies store. He needed to get materials for his school project—the moon phase poster!

The store was bustling with people. Siraj darted through the aisles, grabbing a large dark blue cardboard. "This is perfect! It's like the actual night sky! He spun in place, holding it up dramatically before Noor gave him a look. "Okay, okay, I'll put in the basket properly." He also added several sheets of yellow translucent paper, a glue pen, and golden star-shaped glitter to his basket. Noor, on the other hand, chose a set of coloring crayons and a box of multi-colored glitter to her own art projects.

Back home, Siraj carefully unpacked his craft supplies. His mind buzzed with excitement. He couldn't wait to start! "Omar is going to love this!" he thought. He quickly asked his mom for permission and hurried to his friend's house to plan their project together.

At Omar's house, Siraj eagerly explained his vision. "For our poster, I want to make the moon phases glow! We can use translucent paper so that light shines through each phase."

Omar's eyes lit up. "That sounds awesome! And it's perfect because the Hijri calendar is based on the moon. Let's get started!"

MAKING THE MOON PHASE POSTER

The next day, Siraj and Omar gathered all their materials and began working.

Siraj carefully sketched the eight phases of the moon on the dark blue cardboard, while Omar helped cut them out.

"Omar, do you think this crescent looks right?" Siraj asked, holding up his drawing.

Omar tilted his head. "It's a bit too round. Here, let me try."

The two boys laughed as they adjusted the shapes together. "This is going to look so cool when we're done."

"Teamwork makes the dream work!" Omar joked.

After cutting out all the phases, they carefully glued the yellow translucent paper behind

each moon shape, so that light could shine through them–just like the real moon glows in the night sky!

To finish, they sprinkled golden star-shaped glitter all around the poster, making it look like a dazzling night sky full of stars.

As they admired their work, Siraj's mom walked in and smiled. "This is beautiful! Ma-sha-Allah. Noor peeked into the room, holding a crayon in one hand and a cookie in the other.

"Wow the moon changes so much!" she said, staring at the different phases on the poster.

Siraj grinned. "Of course! That's how we know when the Hijri month starts."

A NIGHT OF REFLECTION

That night, as Siraj lay in bed, he couldn't stop thinking about how the moon guided time in Islam. His moon phases poster was more than just a fun project; it was a reminder of the Hijri calendar.

And with that happy thought, he drifted off to sleep, dreaming of the stars and the glowing crescent moon.

LEARNING GEM:

**Did you know that splitting of
the moon was one of the miracles of
Prophet Muḥammad ﷺ?
The disbelievers once challenged Prophet
Muḥammad to show them a sign of his truthfulness.
On a night with a full moon, Allah enabled the Prophet to
split the moon in two. Each half appeared on opposite side
of the 'Abu Qubays' mountain in Makkah! People near and
far, even in China, saw this miracle. The splitting of the
moon is mentioned in the Qur'an:**

{اقْتَرَبَتِ السَّاعَةُ وَانشَقَّ الْقَمَرُ} سورة القمر / ١

(Surah Al-Qamar, 54:1)

**Which means:
The Hour (Day of Judgment) has approached,
and the moon has split.**

CHAPTER 5

THE MOON'S PHASES

Siraj was thrilled to present his project in school. Monday morning arrived, and science class was the first lesson of the day.

When the teacher called on them, Siraj proudly carried the rolled-up poster to the front of the class, with Omar right beside him. Carefully, they unrolled it, revealing the beautiful night sky filled with glowing moons.

Omar held up a flashlight behind the poster, making the moons glow through the translucent paper. The class gasped in amazement.

"Wow! It looks just like the real moon!" one student whispered.

Their teacher smiled. "This is an excellent project, Siraj and Omar. You've done a wonderful job!"

Then, turning to the class, the teacher asked, "Who can tell me why the moon changes shape throughout the month?"

A few hands shot up, but before anyone could answer, the teacher continued, "Let's explore how the moon moves and what it teaches us."

THE MOON'S JOURNEY THROUGH THE MONTH

"The moon moves in a specific orbit around the Earth," the teacher explained. "Each month, it goes through eight phases.

- **It starts as a thin crescent at the beginning of the month.**

- **The crescent grows bigger until it becomes a half-moon.**

- **Then, in the middle of the month, the moon is completely full and shines brightly in the night sky.**

- **After that, it begins to shrink, going through the same phases in reverse until it returns to a crescent again.**

- **Finally, the moon disappears before the new lunar month begins."**

Siraj's eyes lit up. "That's just like the Hijri calendar!" he said excitedly.

"Exactly!" the teacher nodded. "The Islamic months are determined by the moon's phases. A new month begins when we see the first crescent moon."

The whole class smiled as they looked at the glowing moon poster.

"Now," the teacher said, "who's ready to look at the night sky and find the moon's phase tonight?"

All the students eagerly nodded, excited to track the moon's journey just like Siraj and Omar did!

LEARNING GEM:

A Sign of Allah's Creation

Allah said in the Qur'an:

$$\{\text{تَبَارَكَ الَّذِي جَعَلَ فِي السَّمَاءِ بُرُوجًا}$$
$$\text{وَجَعَلَ فِيهَا سِرَاجًا وَقَمَرًا مُّنِيرًا}\}$$

(Surah Al-Furqan, 25:61)

Which means:
"He who placed constellations in the sky, and placed therein a lamp (the sun) and a glowing moon."

DID YOU KNOW?

Sirāj (سراج) is an Arabic word that means a lamp; something that gives light. This word is used in the Qur'an to describe the sun as in the above verse. It is also used to describe Prophet Muḥammad "sirājan munīran" (Surah Al-Ahzāb, 33:46). Here, sirāj is used in a spiritual sense: the Prophet is a source of guidance that illuminates hearts.

After science class, it was time
for religious education. But today
was special. The students gathered in
the auditorium for a video presentation
about the 12 lunar months and the important
events in each one. Siraj and Omar found seats
near the front, eager to learn more about the Hijri
calendar. As the lights dimmed, the screen lit up,
showing the first month:

THE SACRED MONTH OF AL-MUHARRAM

The video explained that Al-Muharram is the first month of the Hijri year and one of the four sacred months (al-Ashhur al-Ḥurum) in which fighting was forbidden in ancient times.

A very special day in Al-Muharram is the 10th day, known as 'Ashura'. Many great events in history happened on this day:

Prophet Musa (Moses) was saved from Pharaoh

Allah commanded the Red Sea to split into 12 dry paths, allowing Prophet Musa, peace be upon him, and his people to cross safely. When Pharaoh and his army tried to follow, the sea closed in on them, drowning Pharaoh and his soldiers.

Prophet Ibrahim (Abraham) was saved from fire

The tyrant Nimrod threw Prophet Ibrahim, peace be upon him, into a huge fire, but by Allah's command, the fire became cool and peaceful, and he was not harmed.

Prophet Yunus (Jonah) was freed from the whale

Prophet Yunus, peace be upon him, had been swallowed by a huge fish as a test from Allah. On the day of 'Ashura', Allah accepted his supplication, and the fish released him safely.

The screen then showed a hadith of the Prophet Muḥammad ﷺ encouraging his followers to fast on this day.

The Prophet ﷺ fasted on the day of 'Ashura' and encouraged Muslims to follow his Sunnah. He also mentioned fasting the ninth day of Al-Muḥarram with it.

Siraj whispered to Omar, "That means fasting on 'Ashura' is a way of showing thanks to Allah for all these miracles!"

LEARNING GEM:

The 12 Months in the Qur'an

Allah said in the Qur'an:

$$﴿إِنَّ عِدَّةَ الشُّهُورِ عِندَ اللَّهِ اثْنَا عَشَرَ شَهْرًا فِي كِتَابِ اللَّهِ يَوْمَ خَلَقَ السَّمَاوَاتِ وَالْأَرْضَ، مِنْهَا أَرْبَعَةٌ حُرُمٌ﴾$$

(Surah At-Tawbah, 9:36)

Which means:
"Indeed, the number of months with Allah is twelve months in the record of Allah from the day He created the heavens and the earth. Among them, four have special rules."

The four sacred months (Al-Ashhur Al-Ḥurum) are:

LEARNING GEM:

A sad event: The martyrdom of Al-Husayn

Years after the Prophet's passing, his beloved grandson al-Husayn was tragically killed in the land of Karbala' in Iraq on the day of 'Ashoura'.

CHAPTER 7

THE 12 LUNAR MONTHS – SAFAR TO SHA'BAN

The second month of the Hijri year is Safar. Some historians say it was named because many people would leave their homes for travel during this month.

The third month is Rabi' al-Awwal—a very special month. Our beloved Prophet Muḥammad ﷺ was born on the 12th day of Rabi' al-Awwal! This month reminds us of his kindness, wisdom, and the great message of Islam.

The fourth month is Rabi' al-Akhir, followed by Jumada al-Ula (the fifth month) and Jumada al-Akhirah (the sixth month). These months were named based on the weather patterns in ancient Arabia.

The seventh month is Rajab, one of the four sacred months. A great miracle happened in Rajab:

THE MIRACLE OF AL-ISRA' AND AL-MI'RAJ

On a special night, Prophet Muḥammad ﷺ traveled from Makkah to Jerusalem and then ascended through the heavens into Paradise—all in one night! This was an extraordinary journey that showed the power of Allah and the great honor of the Prophet ﷺ.

The eighth month is Sha'ban. It is Sunnah to fast on the 15th day of this month. Sha'ban prepares our hearts for Ramadan, and many Muslims increase their worship and supplications in this blessed month.

CHAPTER 8

THE 12 LUNAR MONTHS – RAMADAN TO SHAWWAL

The ninth month of the lunar year is the best of all months. Do you know which month it is?

✨ It is Ramadan! ✨

Fasting in Ramadan

Muslims all over the world, in every country, fast during this holy month from dawn until sunset.

Laylatul-Qadr: The Most Special Night

The best night of the whole year is called Laylatul-Qadr, most commonly one of the last ten nights of Ramadan.

- It is the night when the Qur'an was revealed.
- The reward of good deeds on this night is greater than one thousand months!
- Some Muslims have seen angels or a strong, glowing light on this night.

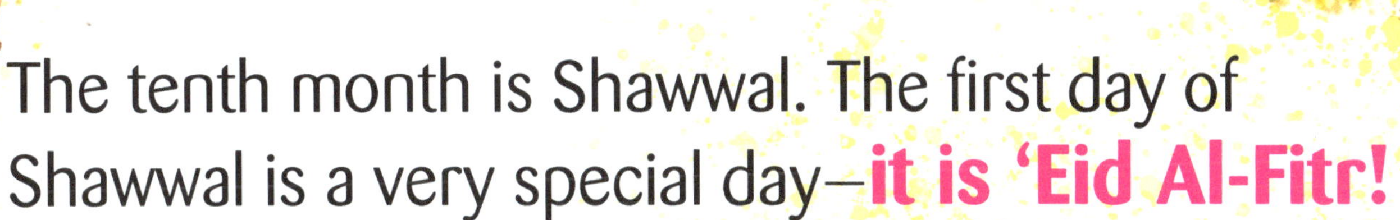

The tenth month is Shawwal. The first day of Shawwal is a very special day—**it is 'Eid Al-Fitr!**

THE JOY OF 'EID AL-FITR

- Muslims celebrate by visiting family, eating sweets, and spreading happiness.
- It marks the end of Ramadan and is a day of gratitude to Allah.

LEARNING GEM:

Battles in Ramadan and Shawwal

The Battle of Badr (Ramadan, 2 AH)

- The first battle between the Muslims and the blasphemers of Makkah.
- The Muslims were only 300, while their enemies were 1,000, yet Allah sent angels to help them.
- It was a great victory for Islam.

The Battle of Uhud (Shawwal, 3 AH)

- This battle took place near Mount Uhud in Madinah—a mountain that the Prophet ﷺ loved.
- The Battle of Battle of Uhud taught the Companions—and us—important lessons about patience and trusting Allah.

CHAPTER 9

THE 12 LUNAR MONTHS – DHUL-QA'DAH & DHUL-HIJJAH

The eleventh month is Dhul-Qa'dah—one of the four sacred months.

The twelfth and final month of the Hijri year is Dhul-Hijjah. This month is very special because:

Muslims from all over the world gather in Makkah to perform Hajj.

• Hajj is one of the five pillars of Islam.

- People of all colors, backgrounds, and countries stand together, wearing simple white clothing, showing that all Muslims are united in their submission to Allah.

The Ka'bah: The First House of Worship

- The Ka'bah was first built by Prophet Adam, peace be upon him, and later rebuilt by Prophet Ibrahim and his son Prophet Isma'il.

- Isma'il, though young, helped his father by passing him bricks to build the walls.

The Day of 'Arafah (9th of Dhul-Hijjah): The Best Day of the Year

- All the pilgrims gather on Mount 'Arafah, making dhikr and supplication.

- Muslims who are not on Hajj fast this day, as it erases sins from the past and future year.

The Joy of 'Eid Al-Aḍḥa (10th of Dhul-Hijjah)

- This is the Festival of Sacrifice, celebrated worldwide.

- Families share meat with the poor and thank Allah for His blessings.

LEARNING GEM:

The Best of the Months

The best month of all is
Ramadan,

followed by:

2. Al-Muharram

3. Rajab

4,5. Dhul-Qa‘dah & Dhul-Hijjah

6. Sha‘ban

LEARNING GEM:

No Racism in Islam
The Prophet ﷺ said in his Farewell Sermon:

قَالَ رَسُولُ اللَّهِ ﷺ:

«يَا أَيُّهَا النَّاسُ، أَلَا إِنَّ رَبَّكُمْ وَاحِدٌ، وَإِنَّ أَبَاكُمْ وَاحِدٌ، أَلَا لَا فَضْلَ لِعَرَبِيٍّ عَلَى أَعْجَمِيٍّ، وَلَا لِأَعْجَمِيٍّ عَلَى عَرَبِيٍّ، وَلَا لِأَحْمَرَ عَلَى أَسْوَدَ، وَلَا لِأَسْوَدَ عَلَى أَحْمَرَ، إِلَّا بِالتَّقْوَى.»

رواه أحمد

"O people! Indeed, your Lord is One, and your father (Adam) is one. There is no superiority of an Arab over a non-Arab, nor a non-Arab over an Arab, nor a white person over a black person, nor a black person over a white person—except through piety."

Narrated by Ahmad

Siraj felt inspired after watching the presentation. He had always known about the Islamic months, but today, he learned how special they truly were.

That night, as he looked up at the sky, he thought about how the moon marks our Islamic months, each with its own special blessings. And then, he began to sing:

"In the dark sky with a silver glow,
The lunar months come and go.

Starting with crescent and then full moon,
We are guided to the month that is coming soon.

First comes Al-Muḥarram,
the first month of the year,
A time to reflect and start fresh and sincere.

Second comes Safar, with lessons and tests,
A time for patience, and to do our best.

Rabi‘ al-Awwal is a month so dear,
When Prophet Muḥammad's birth brings joy
and cheer.

Rajab is the month of a miracle bright,
The Night Journey and Ascension to the greatest
height.

Then comes Sha‘ban, a month of anticipation,
As we prepare for Ramadan with dedication.

Ramadan arrives—a month full of light,
Fasting and worship throughout the night.

Shawwal follows with ‘Eid full of cheer,
A reward for patience and devotion sincere.

Dhul-Qa‘dah and Dhul-Ḥijjah appear,
Hajj unites Muslims from far and near.

The year moves on as we watch the moon,
Guiding us through the months so soon."

SIRAJ OBSERVES THE NEW MOON

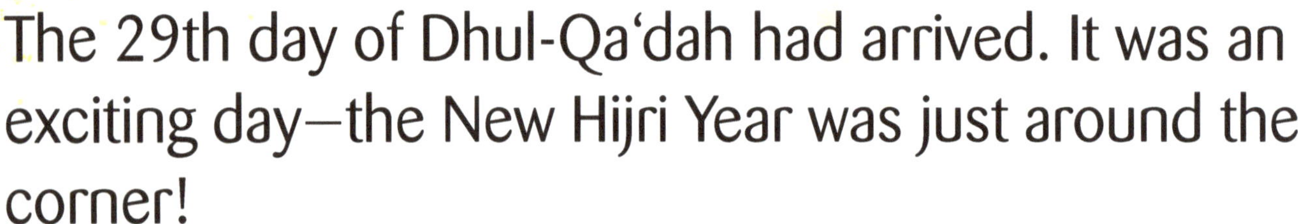

The 29th day of Dhul-Qa'dah had arrived. It was an exciting day—the New Hijri Year was just around the corner!

After school, Siraj helped his mom in the kitchen. They carefully shaped crescent and star cookies from the dough, preparing treats for the school's New Hijri Year celebration.

"How many have we made so far?" Siraj asked, rolling another piece of dough.

"Almost five dozen!" his mom replied, smiling. "That should be enough for your classmates."

As the sun set, Siraj hurried to join his father. They were heading to a hill in their neighborhood to look for the new moon—the crescent that would mark the beginning of the New Year.

LOOKING FOR THE CRESCENT MOON

When they arrived, Omar and his father were already there, scanning the sky.

Siraj squinted upward, searching for the tiny silver crescent. But the sky was covered with clouds.

"I don't see anything," Omar whispered.

Siraj nodded. "Maybe the clouds are hiding it."

They waited, hoping for a break in the clouds, but the new moon was nowhere to be seen.

Finally, Siraj's father said, "Let's head to the mosque for the prayer. We'll find out soon whether the new month has begun."

THE IMAM'S ANNOUNCEMENT

Siraj stepped into the mosque, following the Sunnah of entering with the right foot first. He remembered to say the dua' he learned in the religious education class. *(see learning gem)*

After the prayer, the Imam stood up and announced:

"The new moon has not been sighted tonight. This means that tomorrow will be the 30th of Dhul-Qa'dah, and the New Hijri Year will begin the day after."

Siraj turned to Omar. "So, we have one more day left in this year before Al-Muharram starts!"

Omar grinned. "That means more cookies to enjoy!"

They both laughed as they walked home with their fathers, excited for the special day ahead.

As they strolled back, Siraj happily sang a little tune, tapping his fingers against his pocket:

His father chuckled. "That's a great way to welcome the new year, Siraj."

Siraj smiled. Tomorrow would be the last day of the year, and after that, a new journey would begin.

He couldn't wait!

LEARNING GEM:

The Dua' for Entering and Leaving the Mosque

Siraj and his father stepped into the mosque, following the Sunnah of entering with the right foot first. He remembered to say the du'a he learned in religious education class.

Enter the Mosque with your right foot saying:

اللَّهُمَّ افْتَحْ لِي أَبْوَابَ رَحْمَتِكَ.

Narrated by Muslim

Which means:
"O Allah, open for me the doors of Your mercy."

After the prayer, Siraj and his father left the mosque, stepping out with their left foot first while saying the du'a.

Leave the Mosque with your left foot saying:

اللَّهُمَّ إِنِّي أَسْأَلُكَ مِنْ فَضْلِكَ.

Narrated by Muslim

Which means:
"O Allah, I ask You for Your blessings."

CHAPTER 11

THE NEW HIJRI YEAR CELEBRATION AT SIRAJ'S SCHOOL

Siraj woke up full of excitement. Today was the New Hijri Year Celebration at school!

He carefully placed on his head the colorful kufi his parents had brought him from their Hajj trip. He admired its beautiful patterns in the mirror and smiled remembering the dua' of looking at the mirror he learned at the religious education class.

LEARNING GEM:

The Dua' for Looking in the Mirror

الْحَمْدُ لِلَّهِ، اللَّهُمَّ كَمَا حَسَّنْتَ خَلْقِي فَحَسِّنْ خُلُقِي.

Narrated by Ahmad

Which means:
"All praise is due to Allah. O Allah, just as You have made my appearance beautiful, make my character beautiful too."

As he grabbed his schoolbag, he almost forgot the big box of crescent and star cookies!

"Don't forget these!" his mom reminded him with a laugh.

"Thanks, Mom!" Siraj grinned, carrying the cookies carefully as he hurried out the door while saying the dua' of leaving the house.

A SPECIAL ASSEMBLY

At school, the whole school gathered for a big assembly in the auditorium.

The assembly began with the recitation of a chapter from the Qur'an. A student with a beautiful voice recited, and the room fell silent in awe. Then, a speaker came on stage and told the story of the Prophet's migration (al-Hijrah) from Makkah to al-Madinah with his companion, Abu Bakr.

Siraj listened closely. The story was full of amazement, courage, and inspiration—how the Prophet ﷺ and Abu Bakr hid in a cave, how Allah protected them, and how they arrived in Al-Madinah, welcomed with love and joy.

Then came Siraj's favorite part: the nasheed performance!

A group of students stood on stage chanting the famous madeeh,

Siraj stood among them, drumming joyfully on his drum, keeping the rhythm as the voices rose in harmony.

FESTIVITIES IN THE CLASSROOM

The celebrations continued in the classrooms.

Each student received a colorful, decorated crescent with their name on it and pinned it onto a big board shaped like the night sky.

Siraj beamed with joy as he found his crescent shining beside his friends' names. Looking at the board, he felt a deep sense of belonging—not just to his school but to something even bigger.

"I am part of a much greater family," he thought. "A family of Muslims all over the world united by our love for Allah and His Prophet."

By the end of the day, Siraj felt truly blessed—a proud Muslim kid, ready to start the new Hijri year with faith and gratitude.

LEARNING GEM:

The Story of Al-Hijrah

Prophet Muḥammad ﷺ was born in Makkah and lived there until he was 53 years old. Then, Allah ordered him to migrate to Al-Madinah.

- **The blasphemers of Makkah planned to kill the Prophet, but Allah protected him.**

- **The Prophet went to the house of his companion, Abu Bakr, before beginning the journey.**

- **Asma', the daughter of Abu Bakr, prepared food for them.**

- **They first stayed in a cave near Makkah called Ghar Thawr for three days.**

- A tree grew near the entrance of the cave, covering it.

• **Two wild pigeons nested there.**

• **A spider spun its web across the entrance.**

When the blasphemers reached the cave, they saw the web and the pigeons' nest and thought no one was inside, so they left!

◆ **The Prophet and Abu Bakr then continued their journey to al-Madinah, riding camels.**

◆ **The Muslims in al-Madinah had been eagerly waiting for the Prophet's arrival.**

• Every day, they went outside the city, hoping to see him.

• When he finally arrived, they were overjoyed!

• The Prophet ﷺ let his camel choose the place where his mosque would be built, and it stopped in a humble open area which became the Prophet's Mosque (Al-Masjid An-Nabawiyy).

◆ **The Prophet united the immigrants from Makkah (the Muhajirun) with the Muslims of Al-Madinah (the Ansar), making them brothers.**

◆ **Islam grew stronger after the Hijrah, and the message of Islam spread far and wide.**

🌙 A BEAUTIFUL ENDING

The New Hijri Year had begun, bringing new blessings, new opportunities, and a fresh start.

That night, Siraj sat by his window, gazing up at the night sky. A thin silver crescent had finally appeared—a sign of the new Hijri year. He recited the supplication for seeing the new moon and then whispered a quiet dua':

"O Allah, bless this year with goodness, faith, and happiness for Muslims around the world."

A warm feeling filled Siraj's heart. It was the start of a new journey, a new year and countless blessings to come.

LEARNING GEM:

The Dua' For Seeing the Crescent:

اللَّهُ أَكْبَرُ، اللَّهُمَّ أَهِلَّهُ عَلَيْنَا بِالأَمْنِ وَالإِيمَانِ، وَالسَّلامَةِ وَالإِسْلامِ، وَالتَّوْفِيقِ لِمَا تُحِبُّ وَتَرْضَى، رَبُّنَا وَرَبُّكَ اللَّهُ.

Which means:
Allah is the Greatest. O Allah, bring it over us with security and faith, peace and Islam, and guidance to what You accepts. Our Lord and your Lord is Allah."

(Narrated by Ibn Hibban)